"~~New~~ BAD Girl In Town"

Lost?

I'm Derek, this is Kimberly and Tim.

"Prayer Club?" Oh, no!

Not Bible bangers!

I want no **holy rollers** dogging me!

What set her off?

Got a rep to maintain!

Derek looks **mighty** fine.

Y'know, it just might be **fun** --

-- to **reel in** a choir boy!

Class, welcome **Serenity Harper** from Los Angeles.

Just shoot me...

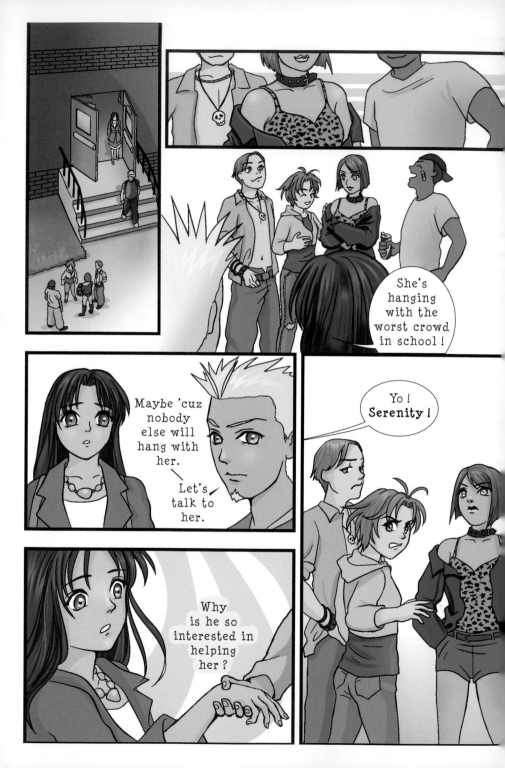

I hate it when you're right.

Bad news, Serenity. You're going to **really** hate this.

You are our new pet project!

No matter how obnoxious you act --

-- No matter how crude you talk --

-- We'll still be your friends.

That doesn't mean we'll tolerate rude behavior or wrong doing.

Screw up, we'll let you know about it.

But if you need help . . .

. . . or somebody to talk to . . .

. . . we'll be there.

HA-HA-HA-HA-HA

@#$%&
it's **NOT FUNNY**!

It is when it happens to **you**!

Relax, it isn't bleeding.

Well, it @#$%& hurts!

Cussin' won't make it feel better.

Shut the @#$%& up!

Child, what happened in there?

Whaddya think happened?

That old @#$%& HATES me!

I agree.

MS BAXTE

Huh? You do?

Mr. Pyle is hopelessly mired in outdated Eurocentric masculine precepts!

Escaped detention already?

Didn't go.

I talked to Ms Baxter instead.

Hey, Serenity, don't let the Pyle-Driver get you down.

...uh-oh...

Next morning...

Maybe she's got a point. Why is bad language "bad"?

Granted, say, "God" or "Jesus" too much . . .

. . . you end up **trivializing** them.

The **N-word** is pretty awful!

But it **isn't** obscene.

Moron -- you just locked yourself out!

No keys, no money!

It's freezin'! * But I can't go back --

* Actually, only 68°

Mom would have to let me in. I don't want her gloating!

Can't go anywhere ... got no friends ... can't go back ...

Huh, Kimberly's church ...

YOUTH GROUP TONITE

I don't wanna go ... but they did invite me ... and it's **warm**!

Nah -- why hang with a buncha Bible-banging losers?

'Sides, I'm not dressed -- they'd laugh at me or get offended ...

That's **it**! If I tick 'em off --

-- they'll never bug me again !

In First Corinthians, Paul wrote on marriage and divorce --

Yo ! Youth group ?

Welcome. You're Serenity, right ? My daughter Kimberly mentioned a new girl.

Later...

I argued all night -- they'll never want me back!

Well, Serenity, your ideas certainly were . . . uh . . . interesting.

Your fashion sense is interesting, too.

Most people wouldn't be stylish enough to come barefoot to church.

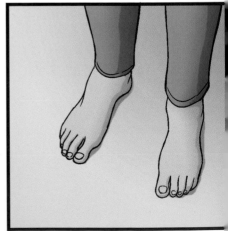

What-**eh**-vah !

As long as you're willing to listen, there's hope.

"Hope ?"

My life's a joke that I'm not in on. Nobody cares !

God cares.

That's the biggest joke of all.

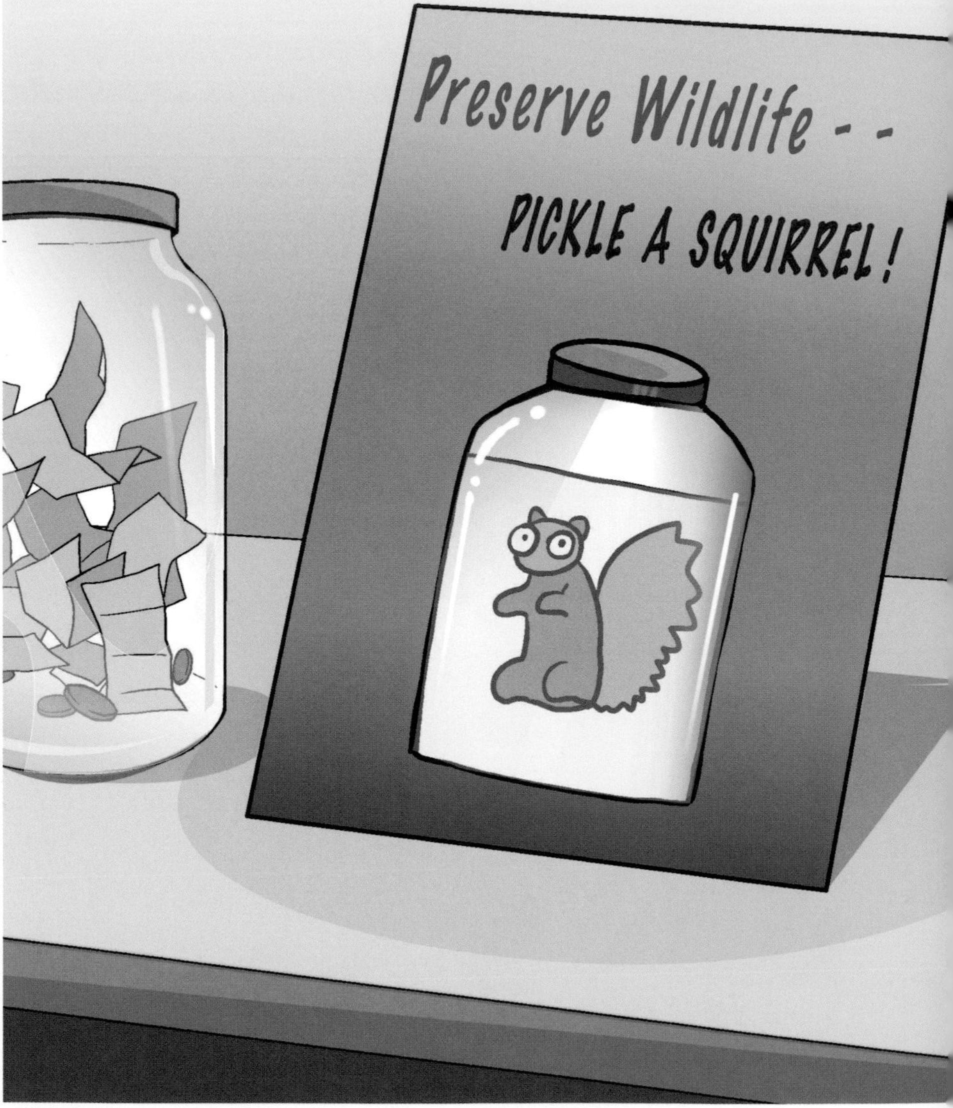
Preserve Wildlife - -
PICKLE A SQUIRREL!

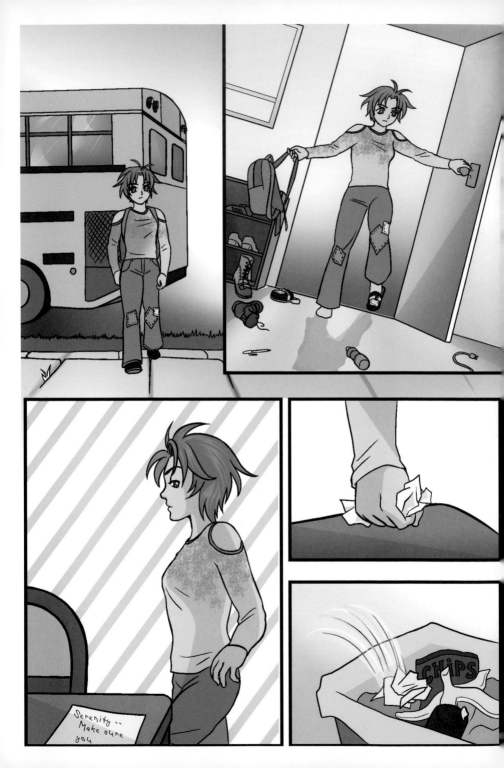

Look, I better go . . .

Hey! You just got here!

Afraid Kimberly might say something?

No, 'cuz nothing's gonna happen she might have something to say about!

If I could figure that out, I wouldn't need help in algebra!

And I'll welcome you as a friend...nothing more, nothing less!

This isn't Christian, but --

-- if Serenity wants Derek, she's got a WAR!

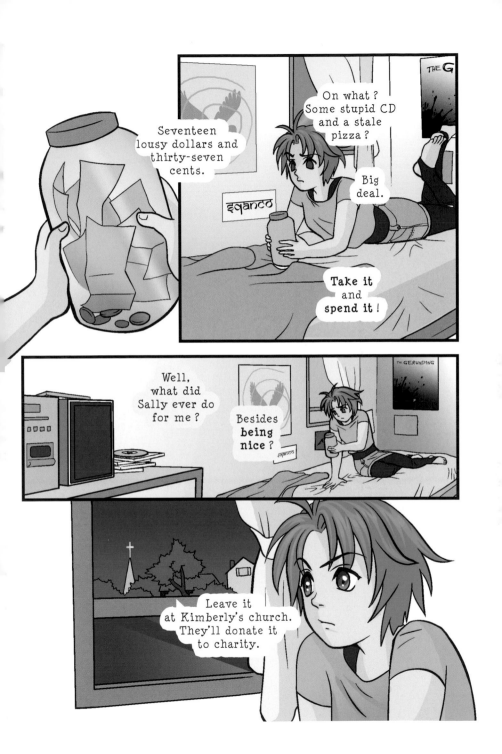

Yeah, but people gave this money to the animal shelter.

Is it **still stealing** if I give the money to somebody else?

Seventeen dollars and thirty-seven cents - -

- - what could they get with that?

Whatever, it'll mean more to them than a cold pizza to me!

Back this
way, officer.
I heard him
jump on the
dumpster!

Yikes!
Better stay
hidden until
they leave...

He
couldn't
have
gotten
far!

...then I
can sneak home...
...shower...sleep...
snzzzzzzzzzzz

Huh?
Wuzzat?

Life's a beach --
come and play!

GOOFYFOOT GURL

You can find
anything on a beach
-- especially FUN
and ROMANCE!

Making her splash in Summer 2007!

Created by Realbuzz Studios
Published by Thomas Nelson
Find out more at
www.RealbuzzStudios.com

Wanna see?
Turn the page for a
SPECIAL SNEAK
PREVIEW !!!

THE revolve TOUR

We're Coming to a City Near You!
TOUR DATES

Columbus, OH
September 14 - 15, 2007

Dallas, TX
September 21 - 22, 2007

Hartford, CT
September 28 - 29, 2007

St. Louis, MO
October 5 - 6, 2007

Anaheim, CA
October 12 - 13, 2007

Sacramento, CA
October 19 - 20, 2007

Philadelphia, PA
November 2 - 3, 2007

Minneapolis, MN
November 9 - 10, 2007

Portland, OR
November 16 - 17, 2007

Atlanta, GA
November 30 - Dec. 1, 2007

Orlando, FL
January 25 - 26, 2008

Charlotte, NC
February 1 - 2, 2008

Denver, CO
February 15 - 16, 2008

Houston, TX
February 22 - 23, 2008

Hawk Nelson

Natalie Grant

KJ-52

Max & Jenna Lucado

Ayiesha Woods

Chad Eastham

Kimiko Soldati

Download **Preview Video** Online

To register by phone, call 877-9-REVOLVE or online at REVOLVETOUR.COM

Serenity

Created by Realbuzz Studios, Inc.
Min Kwon, Primary Artist

Serenity throws a big wet sloppy one out to:
Art G., Stan L., Dana M., Drigz A.,
Cristina dLS, Linda B., Kimberly B., Michael K.,
Bobby & Heather Lee D., Geoff S., Kathleen W., Nate B.,
'n' the CCAL, Biola, and Hampton's posses.

Smack!
Luv U Guyz !!!

©&TM 2007 by Realbuzz Studios   ISBN 978-1-59554-383-7
www.Realbuzz Studios.com
www.SerenityBuzz.com

This book is a work of fiction. Names, characters, places, and incidents are either products of the author's imagination or used fictitiously. Any similarity to actual people, organizations, and/or events is purely coincidental.

Published by Thomas Nelson, Inc. Nashville, TN 37214 www.thomasnelson.com

Library of Congress Cataloguing-in-Publication Data
Applied For

Scripture quotations marked NCV are taken from
The Holy Bible, New Century Version®. NCV®.
Copyright © 2001 by Nelson Bibles.
Used by permission of Thomas Nelson. All rights reserved.

Printed in Singapore.
5 4 3 2 1